Hold My Hand

Hold My Hand

by Charlotte Zolotow
Pictures by Thomas di Grazia

Harper & Row, Publishers • New York, Evanston, San Francisco, London

HOLD MY HAND

Text copyright © 1972 by Charlotte Zolotow
Illustrations copyright © 1972 by Thomas di Grazia

LIBRARY OF CONGRESS CATALOG CARD NUMBER: 72-76506
TRADE STANDARD BOOK NUMBER: 06-026951-0
HARPERCREST STANDARD BOOK NUMBER: 06-026952-9

Hold My Hand

Dark dark dark
black clouds and the wind sighs.
We walk together
you and I
and it's grey and black
and the wind sighs.

How cold it is!
Oh hold my hand.

The wind stops.
Everything is still.
There is only the cold
cold cold cold.
Oh hold my hand.

I look at you
and suddenly the air
is full of snow.

The snowflakes cling
like bits of ice
to our mittens.

Look!
The dried grass is tipped with white.
Everything is light
and cold.

We walk together
through the snow.

It's on your hat.
It's in your hair.
It's on your scarf.
Your cheeks are red.

But oh it's cold
white and bright and cold.
Oh hold my hand!